BASIL
THE GREAT MOUSE DETECTIVE

Based upon The Walt Disney Company's
film of the same name

Hippo Books
Scholastic Publications Limited
London

Scholastic Publications Ltd.,
10 Earlham Street, London WC2H 9RX, UK

Scholastic Inc.,
730 Broadway, New York, NY 10003, USA

Scholastic Tab Publications Ltd.,
123 Newkirk Road, Richmond Hill,
Ontario L4C 3G5, Canada

Ashton Scholastic Pty. Ltd.,
PO Box 579, Gosford, New South Wales,
Australia

Ashton Scholastic Ltd.,
165 Marua Road, Panmure, Auckland 6,
New Zealand

This edition first published by Scholastic Publications Limited,
1986, by arrangement with The Walt Disney Company

ISBN 0 590 70595 4

Made and printed by Mateu Cromo, Madrid

Typeset in Plantin by Keyline Graphics, London NW6

Olivia Flaversham was having a birthday! When you're a small girl, that's wonderful enough, but when your father is the best toymaker in Britain, it is especially exciting.

Little Olivia barely had time to look at the beautiful ballerina that her father had made for her, when suddenly there was a loud pounding at the door.

"Now, you hide in there, and don't come out!" said Mr Flaversham in a frightened voice, pointing to a small cupboard.

Poor Olivia! Looking through a crack in the door, she saw a fearsome, peg-legged bat come crashing through the window. As her father and the intruder fought, a table overturned, trapping her inside the cupboard.

When Olivia finally managed to free herself from her hiding place, she found the room was all topsy-turvy . . . and her father had gone. "Daddy! Daddy! Where are you?" she cried, as she ran to the open window and looked out into the dark night.

Sometime later, Dr David Q. Dawson, a rather portly gentleman who had just retired from Her Majesty's sixty-sixth regiment and was looking for a quiet place to stay in London, discovered Olivia inside an old boot, sitting on a box and sobbing.

After handing her his handkerchief, Dr Dawson was finally able to get the little girl to tell him why she was so unhappy. She showed him a clipping from a newspaper that said, "Famous Detective Solves Baffling Disappearance." Then she explained, "I must find Basil of Baker Street."

"Well," said the good doctor, "I don't know any Basil, but I do remember where Baker Street is. Come with me. We'll find this Basil chap together." And the two friends set off in the rain.

They soon arrived at a small door at 221 Baker Street. Mrs
Judson, the kindly housekeeper, let them in and soon
afterwards they were introduced to the Great Mouse
Detective himself.

   At first, it seemed as if Olivia would not be able to
persuade Basil to help her. Then she revealed the identity of
her father's kidnapper! At last Basil sat up and took notice,
for he knew the peg-legged bat well.

"That bat, one Fidget by name," he explained, "is in the employ of the horror of my every waking moment . . . the wicked Professor Ratigan! He's a genius twisted for evil, the Napoleon of crime. For years I've tried to capture him, but he has successfully evaded my grasp."

And so, Basil of Baker Street agreed to help Olivia Flaversham find her missing father.

Meanwhile, in his lair, Professor Ratigan was trying to force Mr Flaversham to build a clockwork robot, but the gentle toymaker rebelled. Threats were useless. "You can do what you want with me," he nobly declared, "I won't be a part of this evil any longer."

But Ratigan was even more evil than Mr Flaversham
thought. He sent Fidget to bring back Olivia, to persuade the
poor man to carry on helping him, as well as some more
equipment to complete his monstrous, but as yet unrevealed,
scheme.

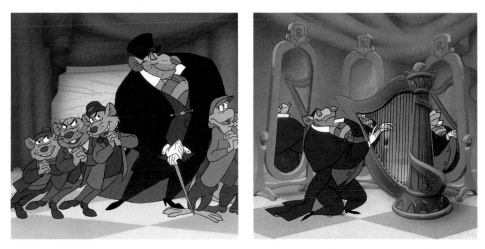

To fill in the time before his plot could be made public, Ratigan decided to have a party with the rest of his gang. The celebration was momentarily interrupted when Bartholomew, a poor mouse who had had too much to drink, sang, "To Ratigan, the world's greatest *rat*!"

Of all the things that Ratigan couldn't stand, being called a "rat" was at the top of the list.

The master criminal went to the door of his lair and rang a small, golden bell. From out of the shadows came the biggest, ugliest cat ever to walk the streets of London. Her name was Felicia, and she loved nothing better than to eat mice. Ratigan held the still singing Bartholomew out to Felicia. With one large, satisfied, gulp she put a stop to the drunken fellow's song.

"Did Daddy's little honeybun enjoy her tasty treat?" cooed Ratigan as he petted Felicia.

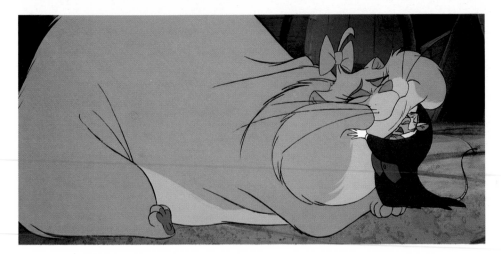

Although Fidget had escaped, he had left his hat behind. Meanwhile, back at Baker Street, Basil was still wondering how he could tackle the problem of the missing toymaker, when he spied Fidget at the window. "Quickly, Dawson!" he cried. "We've not a moment to lose!" The two of them ran out of the house hot on Fidget's tail, but the bat was gone.

What a wonderful clue that provided for Basil's faithful
assistant, Toby the hound. With the dog's help, Basil,
Olivia, and Dr Dawson tracked the peg-legged bat to a

14

London toy shop where they discovered the strangest thing. Fidget had removed the gears and the uniforms from many of the mechanical toys.

    While Basil was trying to work out what lay behind this odd behaviour, Fidget sprang from inside a doll's pram and grabbed hold of poor Olivia. Although Basil and Dr Dawson tried their best, chasing him madly through the forest of toys, Fidget managed to escape with the little girl tucked securely in his sack.

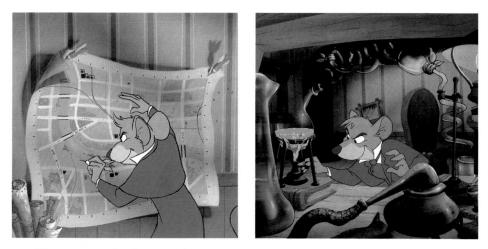

Fortunately for Basil, Fidget was very forgetful. He had left Professor Ratigan's list behind him. Basil read the note, which Dr Dawson had found. "Dawson, you've done it!" he exclaimed. "This list is precisely what we need. Quickly now, back to Baker Street!" Jumping on Toby's back, the two friends rushed back home, where a series of experiments revealed the location of Ratigan's hideout.

But during this time, Ratigan had been far from idle. Showing Mr Flaversham that he had Olivia in his power, he forced the poor toymaker to work harder and faster. When Fidget told the Professor that he had lost the list, Ratigan became so angry he started to feed the bat to Felicia. Suddenly he stopped. By leaving the list behind, Fidget had presented him with a unique opportunity to trap Basil . . . .

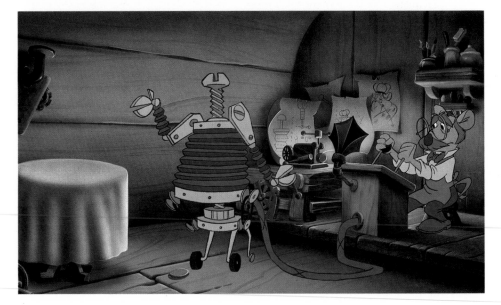

Now that Basil knew that Ratigan's lair could only be on the Thames riverfront, the Great Detective and Dr Dawson set out on the trail once more. Disguised as pirates, they entered a local pub in the hope of finding out more information.

When Fidget appeared at the same pub, Basil was
delighted. His theory had been proved right. The two heroes
followed the peg-legged bat through a maze of pipes into
Ratigan's trap.

Oh, how Ratigan gloated over his achievement! "Isn't it clear to you that the superior mind has triumphed?" screamed the evil rat. "I've won!" His gloating was almost too much for poor Basil, who was so depressed that he was ready to give up.

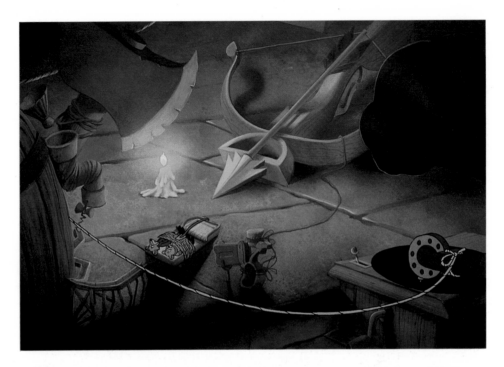

Ratigan had set up an ingenious system to rid himself of
Basil forever. The unfortunate detective and Dr Dawson
were tied to a mousetrap, where they were surrounded by a
gun, a crossbow, an axe and an anvil. All of the weapons were
set to go off at the end of a special song on the record player.
But the Professor had no time to wait to see the end himself.
He left in a dirigible, powered by Fidget's furious pedalling.

Just when it seemed the end was near, Dr Dawson suc-
ceeded in jollying Basil out of his depression. It gave the
Great Mouse Detective just enough time to find a way out of
the deadly trap.

"Dawson, at the exact moment I tell you, you must release
the triggering mechanism!" shouted Basil. And as the Great
Detective had calculated, all the weapons cancelled each
other out and they were free.

In the meantime Ratigan had revealed the true nature of his scheme. Ratigan's men had replaced the Queen's guards at Buckingham Palace. The Professor then replaced the Queen herself with a clockwork double built by Mr Flaversham.

The fake Queen went out in public to proclaim that Ratigan had become her new consort, and from this time on would rule the Kingdom. What a sad day for mousedom!

Just as Fidget was preparing to throw the hapless Queen to Felicia, Basil arrived to rescue her. Toby, delighted to have some fun, chased Felicia straight towards the Palace Guard Dogs, while the Great Detective swore to stop Ratigan once and for all.

Basil wrestled control of Mr Flaversham's clockwork double from Ratigan's men, and turned the tables on the evil Professor. He denounced him publicly for what he was, "You, Professor, are none other than a foul stentus rodentus, commonly known as a *sewer rat!*"

Ratigan thought he had got away safely. But Olivia told him that he was doomed. "Just wait! Basil's smarter than you. He's not afraid of a big, old, ugly rat like you!" The villain pushed the little girl against the side of the dirigible's gondola, but as if to prove her right, at that very moment, Basil's balloon appeared beside him.

The Professor was furious. He led Basil on a frantic chase across the skies of London. Hoping to lighten the load, he even threw Fidget overboard. But it was no use. Ratigan could not shake off Basil, and soon the Great Detective jumped into the gondola to confront his enemy face to face.

Ratigan screamed in rage. His plan had collapsed. But before he could be captured by the guards, he managed to grab hold of Olivia, and escape in his dirigible. Basil, Dr Dawson and Mr Flaversham followed in an improvized balloon.

Then, at that very moment, the craft crashed into Big Ben. Deep inside the gears of the clock the two enemies began their final battle. Basil managed to rescue Olivia from Ratigan's foul clutches and handed her safely to her father and Dr Dawson in the hovering balloon.

   This selfless move almost cost Basil his life. Ratigan, refusing to admit defeat, had crept up behind him, and dealt him a savage blow. The two opponents now fought on the very hands of the giant clock, amidst crashing thunder and blinding lightning.

   As the clock struck the hour, the hands moved, and both Ratigan and Basil fell to the earth far below!

In the balloon they were silent with shock. But suddenly, a squeaking noise made them look up in surprise. There was Basil, pedalling his way up towards them on the propeller of Ratigan's destroyed dirigible, which he had managed to grab hold of at the last second!

Safely back on the ground Mr Flaversham and Olivia said their grateful goodbyes to Basil, and returned to their little home. Dr Dawson, too, prepared to leave, although it was obvious that Basil wanted him to stay.

And then, at the door, appeared a beautiful, young lady in dire need of the help of the famous Basil of Baker Street. The good doctor could hardly say no when Basil proudly introduced him as his "trusted associate, Dr Dawson – with whom I do all my cases."

"From that time on," wrote Dr Dawson, "Basil and I were a close-knit team, and over the years we have shared many cases. But I shall always look back on that first with the most fondness . . . my introduction to the most brilliant mouse I have ever known, the Great Mouse Detective . . . Basil of Baker Street."